ABDO Publishing Company is the exclusive school and library distributor of Rabbit Ears Books.

Library bound edition 2005.

Copyright © 1995 Rabbit Ears Productions, Inc.,
Rowayton, Connecticut.

Library of Congress Cataloging-in-Publication Data

Metaxas, Eric.
  Princess Scargo and the birthday pumpkin / written by Eric Metaxas ; illustrated by
Karen Barbour.
      p. cm.
  "Rabbit Ears books."
  Summary: To save the tribe from the effects of a devastating drought, Princess Scargo
sacrifices her most precious possessions, the miniature fish that live in the beautiful carved
pumpkin she received for her seventh birthday.
  ISBN 1-59197-769-X
  1. Nobscusset Indians—Juvenile fiction. [1. Nobscusset Indians—Fiction. 2. Indians of
North America—Massachusetts—Fiction. 3. Princesses—Fiction. 4. Fishes—Fiction. 5.
Droughts—Fiction.] I. Barbour, Karen, ill. II. Title.

PZ7.M564Pr 2004
[E]—dc22

                                                                2004047316

All Rabbit Ears books are reinforced library binding
and manufactured in the United States of America.

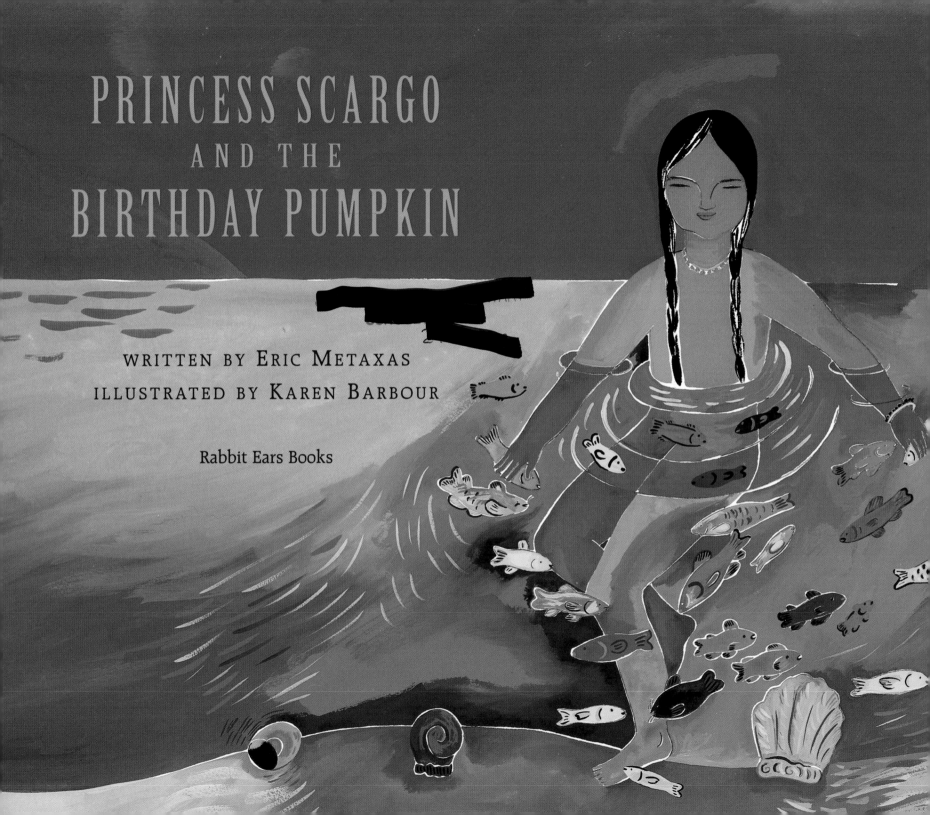

PRINCESS SCARGO
AND THE
BIRTHDAY PUMPKIN

WRITTEN BY ERIC METAXAS

ILLUSTRATED BY KAREN BARBOUR

Rabbit Ears Books

NOT SO VERY LONG AGO, in the days when the curved peninsula that is now called Cape Cod was known as the Narrow Land, there dwelt a tribe of people called the Nobscussets, who were ruled by a great and wise chief named Sagam.

Now, Chief Sagam's wife died in childbirth, and this great tragedy grieved the chief unspeakably. The daughter that his wife bore in her last hours in this world became dearer to him than anything, and so he named her Scargo, which means "new life."

It was Chief Sagam's greatest joy to take his dear daughter for long walks in the forests of their region and, as Princess Scargo grew, she came to greatly love the creatures that lived there, and they seemed to return the affection.

One summer the princess cared for a lame fawn that had wandered into their camp, and the following spring she discovered a fledgling seagull with an injured wing and raised him as her own.

But of all the animals that Princess Scargo loved, she came to love most the silent creatures that darted and glided in the liquid heaven that lay below the surfaces of the shaded ponds and purling rills of her people's land. And it became her secret wish that someday, at least for a short time, she would love and care for some of them in the way that she had loved and cared for so many of the creatures that lived in her own world above the water.

Now, it was the custom in that part of the world for the sachems of neighboring tribes to send presents to the children of other chiefs as a sign of their goodwill. And because everyone knew of the fairness and goodness of Chief Sagam, the gifts that were sent to his daughter, Princess Scargo, were many and marvelous.

One chief sent the little princess an exquisite deer carved from a block of white oak. Another sent her a basket of hollow robin's eggs. But on the occasion of her seventh birthday, in the early springtime, the chief of the Mashpee tribe sent Princess Scargo a gift more fantastic than any other. It took his best runners many days to transport the gift and the fragile cargo that it contained over the many hills to the Nobscusset people.

When it finally arrived, everyone in the village stood staring at it with great awe, for none of them, not even the great-great-grandmothers of the tribe, had ever seen anything like it in all of their lives.

It was a pumpkin, larger and more beautiful than any other, and on its gleaming orange surface was carved in amazing detail every one of the extraordinary animals

 that ran through the forest and every one of the magnificent birds that flew in the hallowed skies above their lands.

And whenever the gold of the sun's rays washed over the orange globe, the slumbering world depicted on its surface seemed for the briefest moment to awaken, and the orange trees shivered as the wind went through them and the orange rabbits hopped and orange birds swooped and lit on orange limbs and orange deer leapt over orange brambles and a clever orange fox ran into its hole.

The princess was overcome with joy at this and, slowly making her way around the pumpkin's circumference, she beheld with rapt interest each one of the creatures carved upon it. But when she had completely circumnavigated its surface, she stopped and a sad look clouded her innocent face, for she realized that nowhere on the vast surface of the magnificent gourd was there a member of the underwater tribe of creatures she had come to love most of all. And she whispered this discovery to her father.

Now, as Chief Sagam was a great
and wise man, and as he knew the
chief of the Mashpee to be a great and
wise man as well, he knew that the
omission was by no means an accidental
one, and so he permitted his daughter to
ask the eldest messenger what its significance
might be.

And when she did so, a smile bloomed on the face
of the chief messenger. With great ceremony he removed the top from the pumpkin
and bade the little princess approach. Although it was nearly as tall as she was, she
peeked in and saw that the interior of the great pumpkin had been hollowed into a
bowl and that the bowl had been filled with water. And there in the glistening pool
swam miniature specimens of every one of the fish that inhabited the lakes and
streams of her father's land.

The sight of this was more glorious than anything the little princess could have imagined. She beheld tiny striped perch and stippled trout and sunfish and chubs and transparent minnows, and pickerel the color of polished brass. There was even a pair

of thumb-sized catfish. And so attractive was the miniature universe they inhabited that, gazing into the magical bowl, it was all the little princess could do to prevent herself from leaping in and swimming among the fish.

Indeed, in the weeks that followed, the princess seemed to inhabit the world inside the pumpkin, for nothing in the world would have pleased her more, and from that very day she seemed to think of nothing else.

Upon arising each morning she would hunt under leaves and logs for grubs and insects and, when she had found enough of them, she would spend the better part of the day feeding the fish and speaking to them in soft tones, and when she did so, she could hear her voice echo as though she were standing inside a great underwater cavern.

But as the spring entered summer and the summer wore on, a great drought came to the land of the Nauset-Wampanoag tribes. The rains of spring had never come, and now the dry summer was setting in. The streams and ponds began to dry up, and the fish began to gasp for air.

The people of the Nobscusset tribe relied upon these fish for their sustenance, and when great numbers of the fish began to die, Chief Sagam called a council. And dressed

in his deerskin robe and skunkskin cap and smoking his carved pipe, he discussed the problem with the elders of his tribe.

After much discussion they decided to undertake the digging of a lake as wide as the flight of the strongest warrior's arrow, one that was large enough and deep enough to withstand the severest droughts the region had to offer. Then when the rains at last returned, it would fill up and provide security against the next drought that might befall their region. But in the meantime the fish population would be nearly destroyed, and there was nothing the tribe could do.

Early the next morning the work began. The strongest warriors of the tribe assembled with Chief Sagam on a knoll and, with the entire Nobscusset people observing, each of them in turn shot an arrow high into the sky. Small boys from the tribe scouted through the scrub pines for the arrows, and, at length, the one that had flown farthest of all was found.

It then fell to Princess Scargo herself, as the chief's only child, to place two large clamshells next to where her father, the chief, stood, and two more clamshells where the arrow had fallen. Thus the lake's boundaries were set.

The eldest squaws wove great baskets from cattails, and then everyone who was able filled the baskets with sand, and the braves carried them to one side of the proposed lake. It was hard work.

The princess saw everyone toiling for the good of the tribe and she wished desperately that she might help. She went first to the old squaws.

"Can I help you weave your baskets?" she asked them.

But the old squaws would not let her, for she was the only daughter of a great chief, and the daughters of chiefs never wove baskets.

She went next to the young braves who were filling the woven baskets with sand. "Can I help you dig?" she asked them.

But they only chuckled amongst themselves because, except for the new papooses in the tribe, she was its smallest member. "You are much too small to help us dig, little princess," they said. And so she walked on.

At last the little princess approached the strong braves who were carrying the baskets full of sand. She watched them groan with the effort. Without them having to say a word, she knew that she was too small to help them.

As the weeks passed, everyone in the tribe continued to work hard, but the fish continued to die in great numbers. This made the princess more sad than can be expressed in words, and she longed more than ever to do something to help. And because there seemed to be nothing she could do, she spent more and more time talking to the fish in the great pumpkin.

Finally, as the leaves began to turn, the great excavation was completed, and shortly thereafter, the heavens opened and the long-awaited waters poured forth. Everyone rejoiced on seeing this, for they had never worked harder in their lives. And over the weeks that followed, they took great delight in watching as the dry hole began, day by day, to fill with water. But still it would take many years for the tribe to replenish their supply of fish, for most of them had perished in the drought.

Chief Sagam comforted his people. "We have given of ourselves," he told them. "And that is all one can ever give. Someday the fish will return."

Princess Scargo was still sad and, as was her daily custom, she walked into the woods to where the great pumpkin stood.

Now, by this time everyone else in the tribe had long forgotten about the pumpkin and the great day on which it had arrived so many months before.

As she stared into the pumpkin at the tiny fish swimming inside it, the princess thought of her father's words. She thought of how much she had wanted to help and of how now it was too late. The job was finished. This made her sadder still. But as she continued to stare at the fish swimming about, an idea came to her. It was a funny idea unlike any she had had before, for the feeling it gave her mingled the sweetest joy she had ever experienced with the deepest sadness. Suddenly, she knew what she must do.

She hunted under leaves and rocks for worms and grubs and, more lovingly than ever before, she fed the little fish who had given her so much joy. Then, in the softest whisper so that no one could hear, not a soul, she spoke to them, telling them of the new home they would inhabit and of how she would visit them there.

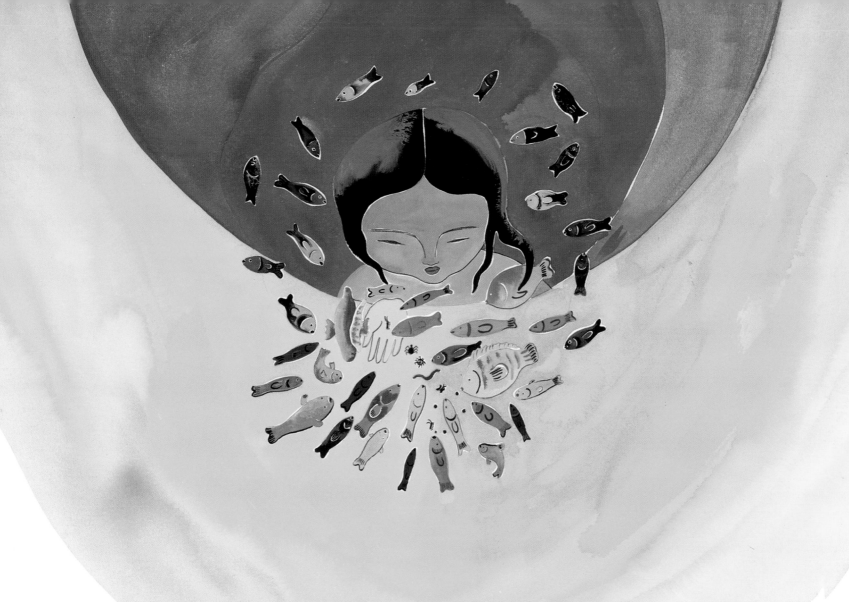

Then, wiping the tears from her eyes, she beheld them in their golden world one last time. When she was ready, she took a pail made of birch bark and, into it one by one, with the great tenderness that is born of love, she transferred her living treasure.

Now, a very strange thing befell the good people of the Nobscusset tribe in the months that followed. For although they could not in any way explain it, the lake that they had so arduously labored to create over the long months of the great drought became very quickly and very mysteriously and very impossibly filled with fish.

And although they did not know why, whenever Princess Scargo swam there, as she often did, she would smile for no apparent reason. And sometimes she would even giggle, as though someone were tickling her feet, which, as anyone knows, was quite impossible.

Now the people of that day are gone, but long after they passed away, the lake that they made during that dry, hot summer remained. It is there even now, this very moment, next to the large, sandy hill that bears its name.

And although few people know of it, there is a legend that says that the fish that swim in Scargo Lake today are the descendants of the descendants of the descendants of a mixed company of fish that once upon a time traveled over the pine-covered hills of the Narrow Land in a glorious orange bowl.